WARTS

BY SUSAN SHREVE

Illustrated by Gregg Thorkelson

TAMBOURINE BOOKS
NEW YORK

Tambourine Books,
a division of William Morrow & Company, Inc.,
1350 Avenue of the Americas, New York, New York 10019.
Printed in the United States of America.

The text type is Bembo.

Library of Congress Cataloging in Publication Data
Shreve, Susan Richards.
Warts / by Susan Shreve ; [illustrated by Gregg Thorkelson]. p. cm.
Summary: Just before the beginning of the new school year, Jilsy breaks out in warts,
and she knows if they don't go away her third grade year will be ruined.
[1. Warts—Fiction. 2. Schools—Fiction. 3. Family life—Fiction.]
I. Thorkelson, Gregg, ill. II. Title.
PZ7.S55195War 1996 [Fic]—dc20 95-51661 CIP AC
ISBN 0-688-14378-4

1 3 5 7 9 10 8 6 4 2
First edition

To:

for stories like this one.

1 ● ● ● ● ● ● ● ● ●

Timbo told me about warts over summer vacation just before I started third grade. He said that when he was my age, he had fifty-six warts: twelve on his right hand and forty-four on his left hand. He had tried to bite them off when the wart medicine didn't work, but they had bled so terribly that our father had taken him to the emergency room.

● ● ●

The night before my first wart, my family had a picnic in my aunt Belinda's backyard. When I went to bed after the picnic, my right hand was normal, as usual. At least I thought it was. But by the next morning at breakfast, a wart had popped up on my thumb. I noticed it when I was eating my cereal—a white bump the size of a fat pea, and quite hard.

"Is this a wart?" I asked Timbo.

He nodded. "Exactly like mine," he said.

"But this is only *one* wart," I said.

"In the beginning, I had only one wart too," Timbo said. "And then I had twelve and then seventeen, and by the end of one week, I had fifty-six warts."

"So what happened when you couldn't bite them off?" I asked, my stomach falling.

"I went to Dr. Breezewood, and he burned them off," Timbo said.

"Oh, no," I said. "Did it hurt?"

"It killed," Timbo said.

"Oh, no," Bam said, squishing a banana in

2

his small fist. Bam is eighteen months old, and he is actually named Samuel. But he can't say Sam, so he calls himself Bam, and we do too.

"Then what?" I asked. "Did they disappear?"

"They turned black," Timbo said. "So I had these little black dots all over my hands, like black chicken pox. Then one morning, they all came back."

"After getting burned off?" I asked. "How come I don't remember this?"

"Because you were only three, and you probably don't remember things well at three."

"Oh, no," Bam said. He loves to copy everything we say.

"Oh-no-what, Bam?" Timbo asked. "Oh-no-Jilsy-has-warts?"

"Oh, no," Bam said again, very pleased with himself.

"Do you have warts, darling?" our mother asked, washing the banana off Bam's face.

"I have one wart," I said. "And I want to get it off today."

"Today?" Mama asked. "Today we are going to the swim club and having a picnic lunch in Gramma's backyard, and then we need to buy you school shoes, Jilsy, and then we have your cousins for dinner. I don't see how we can fit it in."

I looked at my wart in the shaft of morning sun making a rectangular shape across our kitchen.

"Please call Dr. Breezewood," I said.

I don't often cry, not when I fell off my bicycle and broke my arm. Not when I lost Miraculous, the doll I got from Timbo the year I was born. Not when I slipped off the jungle gym in first grade and had to have eleven stitches in my chin.

But I am stubborn. That's what my mother, Annie Rider, says, and my father, George Rider, and even Timbo, who mostly says nothing bad about me at all.

"Jilsy is too stubborn for words," my mother likes to say.

When I was little, I didn't know what "stubborn" meant and asked my father, who is an editor at a sports magazine.

"How can I be something like 'stubborn' if I don't know what it means?" I asked.

So my father looked up "stubborn" in the dictionary and said it meant "obstinate."

I folded my arms across my chest.

"What does 'obstinate' mean?" I asked.

"It means you don't give up," my father said. "And that's very good, most of the time. But sometimes you get stuck in the mud. That's when you're stubborn."

I didn't ask him any more questions, because I didn't want him to look up any more words in the dictionary. But I don't ever remember being stuck in the mud.

It's true that I don't give up. If I gave up, Timbo would be in charge of everything, including me. I love Timbo, but that's the kind of brother he is.

This morning, however, I had to be stubborn about warts—or else, by the day school started, I could have fifty-six of them like Timbo had.

"Please call Dr. Breezewood," I said to my mother.

"Oh, Jilsy," she said in that whiny voice she has when she doesn't want to do something. Sometimes parents are much more whiny than children.

"I have to see him today," I said. "Otherwise I probably won't go to third grade."

I was worried already about third grade, because Ms. Greene is the hardest teacher at Sussex Elementary. Everybody says so. And I'm smart, but only a little smart. Even Timbo, who's quite good in school, had trouble in Ms. Greene's class.

My mother lifted Bam down to the floor and opened a can of Pedigree to feed Cucumber, our basset hound—named Cucumber because she's very long. I think it's a dumb

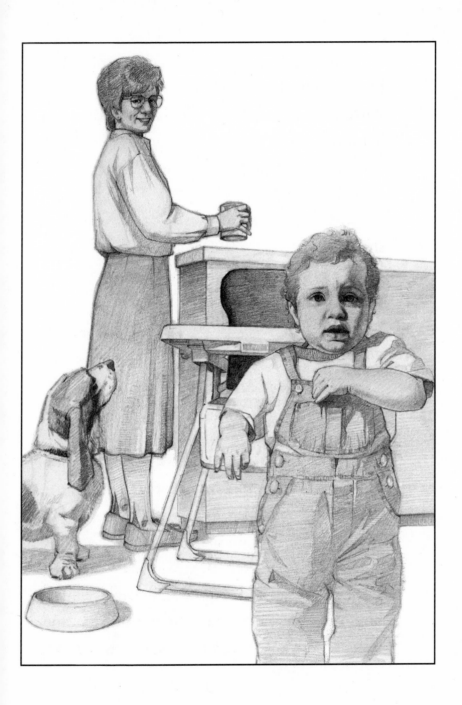

name and so does Timbo, but Cucumber has been around since before we were born, so we had nothing to do with her name. Someday, Mama promises, we will each get to have a pet of our own, and will be able to name it whatever we wish. I plan to get an orange-and-white girl kitten with soft fur, who will have kittens every year, and I will name her Pumpkin. I haven't decided on the names for the kittens.

"Please call Dr. Breezewood," I said again, taking a Lego piece out of Bam's mouth before he choked on it.

My mother changed the laundry and put the dishes in the dishwasher.

"Dr. Breezewood won't be in his office until nine o'clock, darling," my mother said, in her I-am-not-going-to-do-what-you-want-me-to-do voice. "I'll call him then."

I watched the clock, watched the minute hand crawl around the circle of numbers, and at nine o'clock exactly I again asked my mother to call Dr. Breezewood, and she did.

"Hello," she said. "This is Annie Rider. I'm calling to make an appointment for my daughter Jilsy to see Dr. Breezewood...

"I see," she said.

"No, it's not an emergency," she said.

I made a face and jumped up and down and said it was so an emergency, and my mother put up her hand to stop me, but I paid no attention to her at all until she got off the phone and said that Dr. Breezewood was away on vacation.

"Then I'll go see another doctor," I said crossly.

"Dr. Breezewood is the only dermatologist in town, Jilsy."

I happen to know what a dermatologist is, because my father told me. A dermatologist is, a skin doctor.

"Then I'll go to Boston," I said. "There are plenty of dermatologists in Boston."

"Jilsy," my mother said so quietly I could

hardly hear her, "one wart is not an emergency."

"One wart is so an emergency if it turns into a lot of warts," I said, "and that's what happened to Timbo."

"Of course, darling," my mother said, picking Bam up off the floor where he was mushing Cucumber's breakfast in his fat little hands. "Tomorrow, I promise, we will go to Boston to see a doctor if you have more than one wart."

"Okay," I said.

Although I was not entirely happy, I put on my bathing suit, and by the time we got to the swim club where my friends were meeting me, I had almost forgotten all about the hard white wart on my thumb.

• 2 • • • • • • • •

We live in Sussex, Massachusetts, in the United States of America. Sussex is a very small town near the city of Boston, but not near enough to go to the movies or to the skating rink or to the dermatologist.

We live at 4 Beechtree Lane, on a cul-de-sac with woods and a dried-up stream in our back-yard and apple trees in our front yard, and a house painted yellow with white shutters and a bright green door. Our family is well-known in Sussex because my mother works in the children's section of the library and my father is a pitcher for the Sussex softball league. Besides, my mother grew up here and went to the same elementary school that I do, and even had the same first-grade teacher as I did. Her name is Mrs. Paul, and she told me that my mother was very stubborn when she was little too.

In Sussex, our family knows every other family, and they all know us. Sometimes it's very nice. I can go on my bike to the drugstore on Elm Street to get a chocolate milk shake, and if I fall like I did last year and break my arm, every person who lives on Elm Street will offer to drive me home. My mother's parents live in Sussex on Pine Street, and my aunt Belinda lives on Ash Lane, and my uncle Brendan lives in an apartment over the drugstore with his friend Cotton. We don't like Cotton very much because she's bossy, but we're not supposed to tell Brendan that.

My father's parents live in Boston, on a street downtown that has matching brown houses lined up side by side, in a neighborhood where no one knows anyone else.

"I'd like that," my mother said to my father this summer. "I'd love to be a stranger walking down my own street. No one would say, 'Oh, there's Annie in that blue dress that's too tight for her,' or 'There's Annie out today after the stomach flu.' "

"Maybe they say, 'There's Annie Rider with her bad-tempered daughter, Jilsy,' " I said. I am not bad-tempered, but some people in Sussex think I am.

What I am is independent. That's what Mama said.

"What's 'independent'?" I asked.

"I'll tell you exactly," she said taking down the dictionary. "*In-* means 'not,' and *dependent* means 'to rely on someone else,' so independent means 'not to rely on someone else,' " my mother told me. "It's a good thing, Jilsy," she said. "I admire you for being independent."

. . .

"You don't care so much what other kids think about you," Timbo said to me once.

"I do too," I said. "I want people to like me."

"Well, sure," Timbo said. "But you don't care if you're different from other kids. And I do. I want to be the same as every other boy my age. I don't want anyone to notice me too much."

Timbo is quite smart about things. I thought about what he'd said and decided he was right. When every girl in my class asked for a Squeezie doll for her seventh birthday, I didn't. I wanted a blue-and-white baseball uniform with number seven on the back, and a pair of cleats. I really don't like Squeezies, with their rubber arms and legs and fat cheeks and yellow straw hair. I also don't like to wear jeans and turtlenecks in the winter. I'm not at all "girly" as you can tell by the cleats I mentioned. But I like to dress the way my mother sometimes does, in long dresses and tights and clogs. And my ears are pierced with little silver hoops, even though no other mother in Sussex allows ear-piercing until the age of ten.

So I'm a little different, but not a lot.

"You'd be lonely if you lived as a stranger in Boston," my father said to my mother.

"You're wrong, George," she said. "In Boston, I could dye my hair lavender and wear boots to work, and no one would notice."

"I'd like to move to Boston too," I told my mother later. "I'd like to be able to dye my hair blue."

But I wasn't telling the truth. I was very happy in Sussex, riding my bike and going to the swim club in the summer and skating on the pond in the winter. By the end of second grade, I had forty-seven friends at Sussex Elementary. They were all invited to my eighth birthday party on August 1, and forty-one of them came, even though I am sometimes in a bad mood.

Until the morning I woke up with a wart on my thumb, I was perfectly glad to be Jilsy Campbell Rider, aged eight years and twenty-seven days. Then I knew in my heart that I didn't want to be a bit different from anyone else at Sussex Elementary. And no one I knew at school had warts.

• • 3 • • • • • • •

The next morning I woke up early, thinking about warts. It was still dark, so I turned on my bedside lamp to check my right hand. And there they were. Lots more of them—three on my thumb now, two on my forefinger, four on the side of my ring finger, and one on my pinkie. Ten full-grown warts. On the inside of my hand, there was a tiny half-wart, making ten and a half hard, white, wrinkly warts in all.

• • •

I didn't wake my parents. My father is a volunteer fire fighter, so we're not allowed to wake him up too early unless there's an emergency with us.

Like the time Bam swallowed a dime. It was really my fault that he swallowed the dime, since I had picked him up out of his crib and let him play on the rug in my room, where he found the dime and ate it lickety-split. That time, I woke my father up, and we had to drive to the emergency room in Sussex.

But this was not a life-or-death emergency, except to me. So instead I woke up Timbo.

Timbo is always glad to be in charge. So I went into his room, climbed onto the bottom of his bed, and said straight off, in a tiny, frightened voice to get his attention, "You have to help me."

He sat up, turned on his light, and examined my right hand, shaking his head.

"I'm not going to school if I have warts," I said.

"You have to go to school, Jilsy," he said.

"Nope," I said. "I don't have to do anything but breathe."

"Then," Timbo said, "make Mama take you to Boston as soon as she wakes up."

"I will," I said.

"Don't let her procrastinate," Timbo said.

Procrastinate is Timbo's favorite word for the summer and means "to postpone." Mama is always saying "I'll do that tomorrow," which drives Daddy crazy. "Don't procrastinate, Annie," he says to her.

"I won't," I said to Timbo. "I'll make her find a dermatologist, first thing." I dropped down to the floor.

"Did you go to school with warts?" I asked Timbo before I left his room.

"Of course," he said. "I had warts for all of second grade. I had to go to school, or else I would have flunked."

"Did anybody tease you?" I asked.

He shrugged. "A little," he said. And then he gave me a funny look. "They called me Warthog."

"What does that mean?" I asked.

"A warthog is a pig with warts," he said. "I hated second grade."

"Great," I said sadly, and shut his door. I slipped down next to Cucumber, who was sleeping soundly on the rug in the hall.

At breakfast, my father looked up *wart* in the medical encyclopedia.

"Please don't tell me what it means," I said.

"A wart," my father began, pouring himself a cup of coffee, "is a small, often hard, growth in the skin, usually caused by a papillomavirus."

"Hmm," my mother said, cutting up a peach for Bam. "I remember now, from when Timbo had them. Warts are caused by a virus."

"I don't care what causes them," I said quietly, ignoring my cereal. "I want to go to the doctor in Boston today."

"Papillomavirus," my mother said, driving

me crazy, because I could see that now my father was going to look up *papilloma*.

I climbed off my chair and sat under the kitchen table with Cucumber, but my parents were too busy with the encyclopedia to notice.

"A papilloma is a benign tumor of the skin, which contains circular DNA. Do you know what DNA is, Jilsy?" my father asked.

"I don't care what DNA is," I said, but no one seemed to be listening.

"DNA is a substance—it's a kind of chemical code—that exists in the cells of our bodies. Each person on earth has a different DNA. And the DNA code determines how our bodies are formed, inside and out."

And then to my great surprise, I began to cry. Not a little. I cried and cried. I turned over on my stomach and kicked the kitchen table and Bam's high chair and even poor Cucumber by accident. Crying was not loud enough, so I screamed.

"Jilsy," my mother said.

I was enjoying screaming. It made me feel better. I didn't want to stop.

"Jilsy is so dramatic," Timbo said.

And it's true. Sometimes I like to make a big scene, so I do. My mother says it's because I'm in the middle and need attention, but I think it's because I'm a natural-born actress and will end up in the movies when I'm about eighteen.

"Jilsy," my mother said, "I'll call the doctor in Boston, but pull yourself together. You're eight years old."

I don't like to be reminded of my age, as if I don't know how old I am or how a person is supposed to act at age eight. Of course I know. Sometimes I simply don't want to act eight years old at all.

I am not a brat. No one thinks so. Only Mrs. Birdy, my kindergarten teacher, has ever called me a brat—and that was because I spilled the finger paints by accident on Mary D'Amato's yellow dress.

But if I get very upset and no one seems to be paying attention, I flip. That's what my mother calls it.

"Jilsy flipped," she'll say.

Once I looked up *flip* in the dictionary and found that it means "to turn upside down."

"Upside down" is exactly how I feel if I'm upset. So "flipped" is probably a very good description.

4

The dermatologist in Boston was called Dr. Loud. But she had the wrong name, because she wasn't at all loud. In fact, at first she didn't even talk.

She sat me up on a high table, pulled a stool over so that I could see the top of her curly red head, and examined my hands, turning them this way and that way, looking between the fingers and on the palm. Then she checked my knees and my elbows, without saying a word.

My mother finally asked, "What do you think?"

"Warts," Dr. Loud said.

What a genius, Timbo would have said if he'd been there. *Can you believe it?* he'd have asked.

"Yes," my mother said pleasantly. "We thought it was warts."

Of course we thought it was warts. We knew it was. What did she think we were? Idiots, mixing up warts with chicken pox or mosquito bites or measles or any other kind of bump?

"Warts are a virus," Dr. Loud said.

I couldn't remember the word papilloma or I would have told Dr. Loud. But I did say, "I know they're a virus, and I have to get rid of them before school starts."

Dr. Loud nodded. But I knew she had no idea how it felt to be eight years old with ten and a half, now eleven, warts on your right hand when you're about to begin Ms. Greene's third grade.

"There are some options," Dr. Loud said, folding her tiny hands in her lap and looking just beyond me at the wall. "I can burn them off with nitric acid which doesn't hurt—it will cause them to turn black, and then eventually fall off."

"No," I said. "That's what happened to Timbo, and they grew right back."

"I can give you a topical treatment to use every morning and night," she went on, without even listening to what I had to say. "But topical treatments are often unsuccessful."

I shrugged.

I could tell I was making my mother nervous. She was getting smiley like she does if she thinks I'm going to make trouble.

"Or," Dr. Loud said, reaching into a drawer beside her, "I can give you a magic stone."

She handed me a small speckled rock, the

kind I've seen a million times on the beach. It was about the right size to fit in my hand and not show when I closed my fingers.

"Some children with stubborn warts have good luck with magic stones," she said. "Put it under your pillow, and just before you go to sleep, make a wish."

"Like, 'Take away my warts, stone'?" I asked, interested in what Dr. Loud had to say.

"Something like that," she said.

I took the rock and put it in the pocket of my purple shorts.

"I think we should try nitric acid," my mother said, not pleased with the magic stone remedy. "What do you think, Jilsy?"

I shrugged.

"After all, we came all the way to Boston," my mother said. "We should do something."

"I agree with your mother," Dr. Loud said. "We'll try the nitric acid. It almost always works, in spite of what happened to your brother." She got up and opened some drawers, taking out a tray and bottles of white stuff and a long needle and gauze.

I didn't believe her about not hurting, and I was right. It did hurt. She said it would feel cold, which it did. But cold hurts. When you're freezing to death in the winter, and you think your toes are going to fall off, it's awful. I didn't mention the pain. I just concentrated on a man standing on a scaffold just outside the window who was painting the brick building next door.

I knew the nitric acid wasn't going to help. It would turn my white warts black, and then they would certainly show more than they did as plain old white warts. But there was no point in arguing.

I didn't like Dr. Loud, and I was a little mad at my mother for choosing her, instead of finding another smarter doctor in Boston. But I'm only eight, and I can't change the minds of grown-ups.

On the car ride home, I looked at my warts. Already they had changed. Now they were definitely ugly—larger than they had been before I went to see Dr. Loud—fat, wrinkled, white bumps spreading across my hands.

"I hope you feel much better, darling," my mother said.

I didn't answer.

I don't know why she said that. She knew very well that I felt much worse. She's my mother, of course, and knows me better than anyone.

"I like Dr. Loud, don't you?" she asked. "She seems very competent."

"No, I don't like Dr. Loud at all," I said. "I think she's stupid. You know I think she's stupid."

"I'm sorry, Jilsy," Mama said in her sweetest voice. "I know this is an awful time to get warts, just before school starts."

"I know."

"Timbo told you it had happened to him, too, didn't he?"

"He told me," I said, falling silent as we got closer to home.

• • •

Just as we were making the turnoff from the highway into Sussex, I brought up the subject of warts again.

"Mama," I said, in my most reasonable voice, "maybe my warts will disappear by Tuesday, when school starts."

"I'm sure they will, Jilsy," she said.

"But if they don't," I went on in a whispery voice, but I knew she could hear me perfectly well. "If they don't go away, I won't go to third grade."

• • • • 5 • • • • •

My grandmother has a lot of opinions about people. It drives all of us crazy to hear them, especially my mother. But even my mother admits that Gramma is usually right. My grandmother's opinion about me is that I'm too sensitive, just like my mother.

"Sensitive," my father said, getting up from the dinner table to find the dictionary. "Do you know what the senses are, Jilsy?" he asked.

Timbo shot me one of his "Oh, great"

looks, putting his asparagus in his napkin.

I said "Yes" to my father to stop the conversation, but when it comes to the dictionary, my father will not be stopped.

"I know," Timbo said.

"What are the senses?" my father asked.

"I just don't want to say right now," Timbo said, giving me a funny smile.

"Me too, me too," Bam shouted from his place at the table where he had just upturned his plate of SpaghettiOs.

"The senses are the faculties like vision, hearing, smell, taste, and touch."

"I know, Daddy," I said.

"So what does *sensitive* mean, Jilsy?" my father asked.

"Darling," my mother said to my father. Sometimes the dictionary gets to be too much, even for my mother.

"It's important," my father said, and he went right on reading from the dictionary. "*Sensitive* means to be responsive to the feelings of others or to be easily hurt or both," he said.

"That's our Jilsy," my grandmother said.

"Do you know what *responsive* means, Jilsy?" my father asked.

"I don't want to know tonight," I said very nicely, not to hurt his feelings. "I want to eat dinner and then go with Timbo to get a chocolate chip Häagen-Dazs."

"Of course, Jilsy," my father said and, looking at my hands, he added, "I think that doctor did the trick, and you're going to be fine."

But that night after I had inspected my warts under the lamp and read the fourth chapter of *Charlotte's Web* and pulled Cucumber into bed with me, I thought about *sensitive* and knew my grandmother was right. I am very, very sensitive.

If tomorrow were the first day of school and I had a handful of warts turning black, the children in the third grade at Sussex Elementary would not be nice to me. Even though forty-one of them came to my eighth birthday party.

Look at Jilsy Rider's hand, they'd say. *Yuck.*

Don't get close to Jilsy, they'd say. *She has warts.*

My mother says warts are catching, they'd say.

Disgusting, they'd say.

They would make me want to crawl into a hole and sink to the bottom without a trace.

And even if my friends said nothing at all about my warts, I would know what they were thinking, and it wouldn't be nice.

"I hate it when Daddy looks things up in the dictionary," I said when Mama came in to kiss me good night. She laughed a little. Daddy always makes her laugh. "He's so serious," she will say, and then she'll laugh in a way that means she likes him very much.

"I know," she said. "But Daddy just wants to teach you words. He likes words."

"I like words too," I said. "Just not all the time."

She turned on the light and checked my warts and said they were doing exactly what the doctor had said they would do. Then she kissed me good night.

"Alice Hall's birthday is tomorrow, Jilsy, remember? At two o'clock at the swim club."

"I remember," I said.

I didn't tell her I wasn't planning to go to Alice Hall's birthday. I had already thought what it would be like. There I'd be at the swim club with all the girls in my class at Sussex Elementary giggling together on the edge of the pool, and I'd be sitting on my hands hoping that no one would notice the eleven black blisters. But of course they would.

Mary D'Amato would whisper to Alice Hall, *Don't let Jilsy go in the pool with those things on her hand.*

And Alice Hall would whisper to her mother, *Did you see Jilsy Rider's hand?*

And Ms. Hall would call my mother to ask her to pick me up before the birthday cake. *Of course we can't have Jilsy swimming in the pool, Annie,* she'd say.

I wouldn't be able to hear my mother, but

Ms. Hall would say, *I know they've been treated, Annie, but they're warts, after all.*

It was almost ten o'clock by the digital light on my alarm clock. I pulled Cucumber up beside me, hid my face in his stiff fur, and thought about Alice Hall and her mother in jail.

• • • • • **6** • • • •

I didn't go to Alice Hall's birthday party. On Saturday morning, I woke up with seven new warts on my left hand and four new warts on my right hand and the same eleven warts I'd had when I went to bed, only those were very black.

I went into Timbo's room. Timbo was standing in front of the long mirror on his door, checking out how he looked in his soccer uniform.

"Hi," he said.

I flopped down on his bed.

"Do you like number eleven?"

"Nope," I said. "I like number seven."

"Well," Timbo said, "my number is eleven, and I can't change it."

He took his soccer ball down from the closet and put it under his arm.

"Are you playing soccer this fall?" he asked.

"Nope," I said, facedown in the bed.

"Kick ball?" he asked.

"Nothing," I said. "I'm not going back to school."

I showed him my hands.

"Oh, brother," Timbo said. "Just like me."

"Right," I said, turning over on my back and looking at the ceiling of Timbo's room, where the galaxy was pasted and lit up when his lights were off. There was also a big black mark of a basketball on his ceiling, in the middle of the Milky Way.

. . .

"I won't go to Alice Hall's birthday party," I said to my mother.

"That's fine, darling," my mother replied, not at all bothered by the news. "You can do whatever you like these next two days before school starts. The only thing we have planned is a picnic at the park on Labor Day." She kissed the top of my head. I love it when she kisses the top of my head. "I'll call Alice's mother," she said.

After breakfast, I showed her my new warts.

"Oh, dear, Jilsy," she said sadly.

"The stupid stone didn't work," I said. "Can we call Dr. Loud?"

"On Tuesday after Labor Day, first thing," Mama said. "No one's in the doctor's office this weekend."

"Okay," I said.

It wasn't okay, of course. But I decided to be agreeable with my mother, since my plans about going to third grade had changed.

Saturday was a warm sunny day in Sussex, and my mother took Bam and Timbo to the swim club. My father mowed the lawn and clipped back the high hedges that keep us from seeing the Bruners' house on the left and the Hollingses' house on the right. And I stayed in my room to bite off my warts.

In the medicine cabinet, we have a lot of first-aid equipment—long rolls of gauze and tape and Band-Aids and hydrogen peroxide and Neosporin. I got out the first-aid kit so I wouldn't have to ask my father to take me to the emergency room like Timbo did when he bit off his warts. Then I went into my room with Cucumber and sat on the floor just under the open window, so I could hear the whirr of my father's lawn mower while I was removing my warts. I didn't want him to know what I was doing, of course.

• • •

When you bite a wart, pulling it away from the skin on your finger with your front teeth, it comes off quite easily. The problem is that behind the little wart is a long bluish-white stem, which is the root and goes deep into your skin. Biting off the wart is not painful. Pulling the root attached to the wart off your finger, that KILLS. But I was determined.

The first wart I tried was on the inside of my forefinger. It took a while. I pulled and pulled with my front teeth. The root seemed to get thinner and thinner and longer and longer.

Just as I finally yanked out the root and blood gushed all over my hand, my father came in my bedroom. I hadn't even heard the lawn mower stop.

"Jilsy," my father said, very upset. "Don't do that!"

"I did it already," I said wrapping the finger in gauze as tightly as I could, to stop the blood.

"Oh, Jilsy," he said, kneeling down beside me, pulling back the gauze and checking my finger. The small hole where the wart had been was quite deep and filling with blood. He cleaned the wart hole, put on hydrogen peroxide—which stung like anything—and wrapped my finger in gauze again.

"Okay," he said. "Now that's done, why don't we go to the movies? I can do the garden tomorrow."

"S'okay," I said. "I'll just finish reading *Charlotte's Web*."

I didn't want to go to the movies. I know almost all of the children my age in Sussex, and I certainly didn't want to see them this afternoon. Besides, as soon as my father went back to the garden, I planned to continue biting off warts.

But before I had a chance to go back to my room and shut the door, Mary D'Amato called to ask why I wasn't at Alice Hall's birthday party.

"I have a virus," I said. Which was true, of course.

"So does Amy," Mary said.

So I called Amy Fine, who is my third best friend, next to Beth Summer, who moved to Cleveland in June, and Muffin O'Shea, who changed to Catholic school this year. So at Sussex Elementary, Amy is now my first best friend.

"What kind of virus do you have?" I asked Amy.

"I have a stomach virus," she said. "My whole family does. It's disgusting."

"I have a virus too," I said, deciding to test my wart news on Amy Fine. "Warts," I said.

"Warts?" Amy asked.

"They're sort of hard white bumps on your hands," I said.

"I had a wart once on my knee and it disappeared," Amy said. "How many do you have?"

"Twenty-two," I said quietly.

"Twenty-two warts!" Amy screeched in my ear. "Disgusting!"

• • •

And that did it. Amy Fine was certainly *not* going to be my first best friend if I ever started third grade at Sussex Elementary this year.

• • • • • • **7** • • •

I was right about third grade. On Tuesday morning, the day after Labor Day, I walked from my house on Beechtree Lane to Sussex Elementary, arriving at the corner of Ash and Pine at eight o'clock with a stomachache.

I was wearing my favorite faded purple shorts and a blue T-shirt with SUSSEX written in white on the back, new sneakers, and a red baseball cap on backward like Timbo wears.

My book bag had a PB&J sandwich and a plum. The only thing different about me at all since second grade was that I was wearing my grandmother's white gloves.

By Labor Day, I had twenty-six warts—nineteen black ones, four tiny ones, and three bloody holes where warts had been before I bit them off.

"Oh, darling," my mother had said. "You *are* a bit of a mess."

We were in the kitchen, cleaning up after the Labor Day picnic at Sussex Memorial Park. Most of the families in Sussex go every year to play baseball and horseshoes and kick ball and eat chicken and potato salad and yummy cakes made by the grandmothers.

I didn't go.

"I won't," I said to my mother. She didn't argue with me, but Timbo did.

"Get over it, Jilsy," he said. "I went everyplace with warts."

"We're different," I said. "I'm going no place with warts."

My father stayed at home with me again, and we sat on the screened porch overlooking our backyard, reading.

"I might not be able to go to school tomorrow," I said once, looking up from my book.

"I think you will, Jilsy," my father said, very kindly.

"Who knows?" I said, under my breath. But I knew. My parents are not the sort of parents who change their minds.

Some of the children in my class get to stay home from school for nothing. Even Muffin, whose parents are very strict, stayed home three days in second grade because she was overtired. And Mary D'Amato stays home lots, sick or not, and watches soap operas on TV. I'm not allowed to watch TV at all, except an hour on weekends, and I'm not allowed to stay home from school unless I have a fever over one hundred degrees. That's it. No questions. The only time I ever stuck the thermometer under hot water to make my temperature go up, I got caught by my father, and off I went to school in a hurry.

"School is your job," my father says. And Mama agrees.

I put the rest of the chicken in the fridge and folded the red-and-white-checked table-cloth with my mother.

"My hands look too awful to go to school tomorrow," I said, helping my mother clean out the crumbs from the picnic basket.

"I know that's how you feel, sweetheart. But it's the first day of school, and no one will notice your hands," she said to me.

"Yes, they will," I said. "Children notice everything."

She picked up my warty hand and kissed it.

"I wish you hadn't bitten them, Jilsy," she said. "They wouldn't show so much if they weren't bloody."

"Well, I did bite them," I said crossly, and left the kitchen for my room.

• • •

The white gloves were Gramma's idea. She didn't seem to be bothered by the look of my hands, but she was worried about infection.

"With all those holes in your hands, Jilsy, you could get germs."

The gloves were white cotton, small and squarish, not too long on my wrist. You can imagine how I looked on my way to the first day of third grade in my sneaks and shorts and baseball cap and white gloves. But at least my hands didn't show.

My plan was to say I'd had surgery. Emergency surgery on Labor Day. My father had emergency surgery on a broken ankle last year, and it sounded important. *I have to wear white gloves because I had surgery yesterday,* is the conversation I had in mind.

But Mary D'Amato didn't even mention the gloves. When I met her at the corner of Ash and Pine, she was too excited about Alice Hall's birthday party to notice.

"Muffin threw up the cake," she said, to begin with. "It was chocolate fudge."

She told me about the magician who did tricks for the party and was a creep, and the hot dogs, which were mostly eaten by the Halls' golden retriever puppy, and the favors, which were tiny bare-bottomed Squeezies. "There's probably one left over for you," she said.

Elsa Darwin fell off a tree and broke her arm and had to be taken to the emergency room. And Alice Hall had a temper tantrum at her very own birthday party.

"It wasn't so fun," Mary said, eating the cookie out of her lunch box. "I didn't get a good prize at the games."

Amy was sitting on the bottom steps of the school building, waiting for me. We were dressed alike as we'd planned to be, in purple shorts and blue SUSSEX T-shirt and red baseball cap on backward. All except the white gloves.

"How come you have on gloves?" she asked. "'Cause of your warts?"

I nodded. I didn't even get a chance to mention the surgery.

"Warts?" Mary D'Amato said. "You have to wear gloves if you have warts?"

"Jilsy has a zillion warts," Amy said, with one of those looks girls can have.

"But I'm wearing gloves because of germs," I said, feeling weak in the knees, as if I could cry any minute. Then what would they think? I knew exactly. I'd been in school for long enough to know what they'd think and say.

Jilsy Rider's crying like a baby, they'd say, *because of warts. Bumpy, bloody, revolting warts!*

"Who has germs?" Alice Hall asked.

I looked around. Suddenly everyone was there, at least almost every one of the girls in third grade—Alice and Sandy and Mary and Polly and Rose and Franny and Fern.

"You have warts, Jilsy?" Fern asked.

"More than one?" Rose asked. "I used to have one on my elbow."

"Show us," Mary said.

I'm not sure why I took my gloves off then. I knew what would happen if the girls in my class got to look at my poor hands, with their bloody holes and black dots and little white bumps.

And it did. Not right away, but by recess, I wanted to disappear.

• • • • • • • • **8** • •

Everyone at Sussex Elementary was afraid of Ms. Greene, but she was a good teacher. She always had the best class in the school, the hardest working class, the most serious class. Every year children from her third grade won prizes in the county for spelling bees and math-offs and essay contests. She wasn't exactly mean, but she was very strict.

"Even if you're scared of her," Timbo told me, "she's always fair."

She was very tall, and thin as a pencil, with short black hair and large glasses in red frames. She had a way of saying my name, JILsy RIDer, even before she was my teacher, that gave me the feeling she could see straight through my brain to my bad thoughts.

So you can imagine how worried I was to be in Ms. Greene's class with black, white, and bleeding warts hidden in cotton gloves.

Just before the bell rang, I took a seat in the back of the room where the boys sit, hoping to be hidden by the huge curly head of Dusty Frank and the large round back of Nicho Burns.

Ms. Greene's classroom was not decorated like the other classes at Sussex. There was no WELCOME THIRD GRADE sign on the bulletin board, or pictures of each of us on the wall, or even orange and yellow marigolds on her desk. The room was plain and serious and very quiet.

She said "Good morning" without a trace

of a smile. "I'm going to call roll now," she said. "Simply answer to your name."

Other teachers ask us what we did on our summer vacation and tell us how tanned and tall we look. Ms. Greene was not interested in our personal stories. She was only interested in our work.

At least, I thought, she wouldn't be interested in why I was wearing white gloves. And she wasn't. Not at first.

She called the roll, handed out a reading comprehension quiz, collected the quizzes, and divided us into reading groups. She expected us to bring *The Boston Globe* to school every morning, and to read the news in the first section before class.

"It's important to keep up with the times in which you live," she said.

I didn't want to read *The Boston Globe*. The print was small, like the print in the dictionary, and usually the stories were not interesting. But I could tell I wasn't going to have a choice.

• • •

Amy was in my reading group, and Dusty Frank and Mary D'Amato and some others, and they started talking right away while Ms. Greene was working with another group of readers.

"How come you're wearing gloves, Jilsy?" Dusty Frank asked.

"She has a virus," Amy said.

"Is it catching?" Dick Paulie asked.

"Of course," Mary D'Amato said. "That's why she has to wear gloves, so we won't catch it."

"It's warts," Amy said.

"Yuck," Dusty said. "I hate warts."

"Jilsy's warts are black," Alice Hall said.

"And some are bloody," Mary D'Amato said.

I said nothing at all. I was sitting right there with all my classmates chattering away about me as if I were invisible.

At the pay telephone after first period, I called my mother.

"I don't feel well," I said. "Have you called Dr. Loud?"

"Not yet," my mother said.

"I want to go today," I said.

"I'll try to get an appointment," she said. "At least I promise we'll get to Boston this week. It's not an emergency, Jilsy. You're going to be fine."

"I'm not fine now," I said, slipping the receiver back on the hook.

When I got back to the classroom, something had changed. I couldn't tell what, but the room looked different, and when I checked to see where my desk was, it seemed to have moved. I was sitting all alone. Dusty had moved way far forward, and Nicho Burns had moved way over to the other side, and so had Amy, so my poor desk had a circle with no one around it. And Ms. Greene did not seem to have noticed.

"You should take off your gloves, Jilsy," Amy whispered when I walked by. "They make you look a little stupid."

I gave Amy Fine a look, sat down, and opened the math book to page one. Ms. Greene was explaining fractions.

"Nicho," Ms. Greene said. "What is a fraction?"

Nicho was staring at my gloves. I could feel his eyes as if they had popped out of his eye sockets, and were touching my hands. I put my head down on my desk so my hair covered my hands and no one could see them.

"Amy Fine?" Ms. Greene asked.

Amy didn't seem to know the meaning of *fraction* either.

"Dusty Frank?

"Mary D'Amato?

"No one knows what a fraction is, at the beginning of third grade? I'm very surprised," she said. "Jilsy Rider?"

My head popped up automatically.

"Yes?"

I was afraid she was going to ask me what was the matter with me, or didn't I feel well, or why wasn't I listening.

"What is a fraction?" she asked.

"A fraction," I said, remembering, "is a part of a whole."

"Thank you, Jilsy," Ms. Greene said.

And, for the first time in many days, I felt a flutter of happiness in my heart.

• • • • • • • • 9 •

Ms. Greene stopped me before recess.

"I want to ask you about your gloves, Jilsy," she said, pulling up a chair for me beside her.

"I'm wearing them because of warts," I said. My voice was shaking. I hadn't known it was going to shake when I started to speak, and I was embarrassed.

"Warts?" Ms. Greene said. "I had warts when I was your age. I remember exactly when. I was in Mrs. Trimble's third grade."

Mrs. Greene was a businesslike teacher, not the kind of person to tell what it was like when she was a little girl, Timbo had said. So I was pleased she'd told me about her warts.

"Are they so terrible that you need to wear gloves?" she asked.

I nodded, looking around the room to check if anyone was still there, but the room was empty. I took off my gloves.

"These are my grandmother's," I said.

"I certainly didn't think they were yours," Ms. Greene said. "Children don't wear white gloves any longer. But they used to, and I wore them."

I put out my hand for her to see. In the dusty sunlight that fell across her desk, the bloody holes looked almost purple and full of pus, and the black dots smelled of dying skin. I couldn't exactly blame my friends for not wanting to be near me.

"Do they hurt a lot?" Ms. Greene asked unbothered by the awful sight. "I can't remember if mine hurt. It was so long ago."

"Not exactly," I said. "Except these." I pointed to the bloody ones, which were no longer covered with gauze, so they could heal more quickly.

Ms. Greene laughed.

"I bet those are the ones you tried to bite off," she said.

I couldn't believe my ears.

"How did you know?" I asked.

She shrugged. "I know, because I did the same thing."

At recess, most of the girls in third grade were playing Squeezies on the hill next to the soccer field, and the boys were playing soccer. Usually I played with the boys, and so did Amy, and Muffin who had gone to Catholic school this year, and sometimes Alice Hall. I stood on the blacktop deciding what I would do. I felt uncomfortable standing by myself, as if everyone looking at me was thinking, *There's Jilsy Rider, all alone because she has no friends any longer.*

School was hard enough with warts. But recess was harder, and lunch would be the worst.

A first-grade boy whom I recognized asked me why I was wearing gloves.

"Because I'm a doctor," I said, "and doctors wear gloves."

"You're lying," he said, and told his friend, who sat on the jungle gym pointing at me.

"There's Dr. Blah-blah-blah," he called.

Timbo came over in his soccer uniform from the junior high at the top of the hill with Alice's brother, Charlie Hall, and asked did I want to play.

"It doesn't look as if any girls are playing," I said. But I was very glad he'd asked me.

"Jilsy's got warts," he said to Charlie Hall. "That's why she's wearing gloves. Remember when I had them?"

"Yeah," Charlie said. "It was awful." Then he turned to me and said, "I hope you feel better soon."

I wanted to tell him I felt fine every place except my heart—and my heart killed.

I wandered around the edge of the blacktop wishing for recess to be over, glancing at the girls in my class out of the corner of my eye. No one came over to talk to me. I saw Amy walking along with her arm slung over Mary D'Amato's shoulder, and Alice Hall climbing the apple tree with a new girl I hadn't met.

Timbo was playing goalie for the Blue team. I didn't see any girls at all on the soccer field this year.

"Hi, Jilsy," the gym teacher said, coming up the hill, carrying baseball bats. "I hear you've got a bad case of warts."

"Did Timbo tell you?" I asked.

"Not Timbo," she said. "Your friends in third grade did."

I don't have any friends in the third grade, I wanted to say. *They are sitting on the hill right*

now with their stupid Squeezie dolls, probably say-
ing bad things about me. Girls can be unkind.

I was on my way back to the building, planning to tell the nurse I was sick with a virus, when Amy Fine came up behind me.

"Hi," she said. "How do you like third grade?"

"Okay," I said. I certainly wasn't going to tell the truth.

"I hate Ms. Greene."

"Because she's strict?"

"Nope," Amy said, swinging her arms in a confident sort of way. "Because she has bad breath."

"Are you sure?"

"Positive," Amy said.

"I was right beside her and I couldn't tell," I said.

"Your smeller must be ruined," Amy said, laughing.

We were walking along the blacktop by

the first-graders jumping rope, when Amy told me what the third-grade girls were saying.

"They sort of don't want to be near you," she said. "Mary told me that warts are very catching, and her mother told her to stay away from anyone with warts until they go away."

"So," I said, although my heart was breaking, "she'd better stay away from me."

"You've got to admit, it's pretty revolting," Amy said. "Maybe you should stay home from school."

"I can't," I said. "I'm not sick."

"Well, you have a virus," Amy said. "Have you told Ms. Greene?"

"I told her before recess," I said, and then out of the blue, because I was so mad at Amy Fine that I wanted to cook her for dinner, I added, "I'll tell her about her bad breath when I get back to class. She probably wants to know."

"Don't tell her that," Amy said, running up the steps with me. "She'll kill me."

"Maybe she'll get a new kind of tooth-paste," I said, a little pleased with myself.

"Please, Jilsy," Amy said. "I'll be in so much trouble."

I walked ahead of her into the classroom and slipped into my seat.

I certainly didn't like Amy Fine any longer, or Mary or Alice. I was more lonely than I had ever been in my life. Maybe I didn't even like Sussex Elementary, and wanted to move to Boston and live in a neighborhood where I was a stranger.

That night I couldn't sleep. First the light from the street flooded my room, and then the sound of the Bruners' television came through the open window, and then at nine o'clock the telephone rang. I heard my mother say, "Hello, Ms. Greene."

Probably Amy's parents or Mary's mother had called Ms. Greene to say I shouldn't be allowed to come to school. That was fine with me. I was glad to stay home all year.

I heard Timbo padding along the hall and called out to him.

"Did you hear Mama talking to Ms. Greene?" I asked.

"I did," he said.

"How come?" I asked.

"I don't know," he said. "Mama," he called over the banister. "Jilsy wants to know how come Ms. Greene called."

I waited and waited. There was another telephone call, then Mama went into Bam's room because he was crying those breathy little cries of his. Finally, she came to my door.

"Ms. Greene wants you to come to school early tomorrow, darling," she said.

"How come?" I asked.

"She didn't say. She just said she wanted to see you alone before the other children arrived." She kissed me good night on top of my head and lifted Cucumber up to sleep beside me. "It seems fine, Jilsy. Ms. Greene was very friendly. In fact, I've never heard her sound so friendly before, so you must have done something right."

. . .

I waited until Mama had gone downstairs. Then I got up, opened the drawer where I put the magic stone from Dr. Loud, rubbed it until it was warm and shiny, and put it under my pillow.

I don't know why. I don't really believe in magic. But, I thought, why not?

Nothing else was working either.

● ● ● ● ● ● ● ●**10**

When I woke up the next morning to a bright sunny September day and checked my hands in the light, I had two new warts. The new ones were on my wrist and medium-sized: twins, side-by-side warts. I threw the magic stone in the trash can, put on my purple shorts and blue shirt and red baseball cap, put the white gloves in my pocket, and went downstairs.

● ● ●

"I won't eat breakfast if you make me go to school," I said to my mother.

"You don't have to eat breakfast," my mother said, giving Bam a graham cracker.

"But I do have to go to school?" I asked. "Is that what you're saying?"

My mother didn't reply, since the answer was yes, of course, but Bam said, "No no no," banging his spoon on the table.

My father drove me on his way to work since I had to see Ms. Greene early, and he always leaves early because his office is in Boston. Besides, he was probably a little worried that I wouldn't go to school unless he drove me and watched me walk up the cement steps and go through the green double doors.

Ms. Greene wasn't there when I arrived at two minutes before eight and sat down at the back of the room, but she came in just after eight with her arms full of books. She put them down on her desk, said good morning without looking up at me, walked to the back of the room, and sat beside me at the desk selected the day before by Dusty Frank.

"Yesterday," she began in a serious way, "I overheard some of the third-grade girls talking about you as I was leaving the building."

"I know. I heard them too," I said. "They think warts are catching."

"That's what I heard them say."

"But they're not."

"I called the school nurse to check, and you're right."

"Girls can be like that," I said, shrugging. "They can be mean."

"Not in my class," Ms. Greene said. "Which is why I called your mother last night, because today I'm going to ask you to come to the front of the class, while I talk to them about your warts."

Great, I thought. *What a terrific idea,* I thought, my stomach falling. And my face must have turned very white, the color of paste, because Ms. Greene asked whether I was all right.

"Why are you going to do that?" I asked, hoping my voice wouldn't shake this time.

"Because," she said, "when something is different about a child, other children are afraid of her. I've noticed that this is true of grown-ups as well."

"Children want to be the same as other children. That's what Timbo told me."

"But things happen to us, like your warts. We're not perfect, thank goodness," Ms. Greene said. "So I want to talk about warts in front of everyone. Then no one will have the need to talk about you behind your back. You see?" she asked. "The mystery will be gone. Things are much more frightening when they're secret," she said, writing WEDNESDAY, SEPTEMBER 4, on the blackboard.

While Ms. Greene called the roll, I was worried. Worse than worried. I was terrified. And when she finished calling the roll and asked everyone to be quiet, because she had something to talk to them about, I walked to the front of the class light-headed, my knees shaking, feeling as if I were in the middle of a nightmare from which I couldn't wake up.

"Jilsy," Ms. Greene said, sitting at her desk, her large red-framed glasses perched on her nose. I was standing in front of the class, directly in front of Alice Hall's desk, feeling extremely frightened and stupid.

"Take off your gloves," she said.

I don't know what I had expected her to say, but I didn't expect that. I was so surprised I did exactly what she had asked me to do, and took my gloves off and put them in the pocket of my purple shorts.

"Jilsy has warts," Ms. Greene began. "They come from a virus called papillomavirus, which is not dangerous or worrisome or catching. It's not pretty, however, and not much fun."

The children sat stone still in their seats, their

heads turned away, looking down at their desks.

"Any questions?" she asked.

The room was so quiet I could hear my own breathing.

"I didn't like what I heard from many of the children in this class yesterday, particularly the girls," she said, taking my two warty hands in hers. "I don't expect to hear it again."

I don't know what happened next, or how it happened, but suddenly I was the most important girl in the third grade.

"I'm really sorry, Jilsy," Alice Hall said.

Dusty Frank slapped me five as I walked by.

There was a note on my desk from Amy. It read:

I'm sorry!
Love forever and ever
Amy♡
P.S. You didn't say anything
about b. breath, did you?
Love and kisses and hugs,
Amy

At recess, I played soccer with the third-grade boys and Amy and Alice and Karen, the new girl from Washington, D.C. At lunch I sat between Mary D'Amato and Amy, and after lunch, I won the spelling bee.

"I hear that Ms. Greene thinks you're amazing," Timbo said.

"Who told you that?"

"Charlie Hall, who heard it from his sister."

"Actually, she didn't say I was amazing. She said I had warts right in front of the whole class, and then she told everyone not to be mean to me about it, and then she held my warty hands. It was weird."

"She's never like that. At least she wasn't ever like that when I was in third grade," Timbo said. "Maybe she likes you."

"Maybe," I said. "But she also knows how I feel, because she had warts too."

"So third grade is okay after all."

"Okay enough," I said.

• • •

Later that night, after dinner and home-work, and ice cream at the drugstore with Timbo, my mother came in to kiss me good night. I was lying awake in the dark, looking out the window.

"I know it hasn't been easy to go to school this week, Jilsy," Mama said, "but I'm proud of you for going."

I shrugged. "S'okay," I said.

She turned on the light next to my bed, to check my hands. "Dr. Loud called me to say she can work you in for an appointment tomorrow."

"What do you think?" I asked her.

"They look a little better to me," my mother said.

"They look better to me too," I said. "Maybe you should cancel the appointment."

"Are you sure?" Mama asked.

"I think so," I said. "I got asked to play soc-cer for the first team. Alice and Amy and me," I said, "and we start tomorrow."

"Then I'll call Dr. Loud first thing,"

Mama said, kissing the top of my head and turning out my light.

The moon outside my window was full and clear and bright, filling my room with light that turned my covers, and me, and Cucumber sleeping beside me, the color of silver.

Tomorrow, I thought happily, I would ask for the kitten I'd been hoping to get, an orange-and-white girl kitten with soft fur, called Pumpkin.